王华 ◎ 著

海未央

The Boundless Sea

青岛出版集团｜青岛出版社

图书在版编目（CIP）数据

海未央：汉英对照 / 王华著. -- 青岛：青岛出版
社, 2024.12. -- ISBN 978-7-5736-2906-7

Ⅰ. I227

中国国家版本馆CIP数据核字第2025H4C704号

HAI WEIYANG

书　　名	**海未央**
著　　者	王　华
插　　画	张　毅
出版发行	青岛出版社（青岛市崂山区海尔路182号，266061）
本社网址	http://www.qdpub.com
邮购电话	0532-68068091
责任编辑	李　丹
内文排版	戊戌同文
印　　刷	青岛名扬数码印刷有限责任公司
出版日期	2024 年 12 月第 1 版　2024 年 12 月第 1 次印刷
开　　本	32 开
印　　张	5.75
字　　数	150 千
书　　号	ISBN 978-7-5736-2906-7
定　　价	52.00 元

编校印装质量、盗版监督服务电话　4006532017　0532-68068050

2024 年 8 月 拍摄于独库公路

王华 | 山东牟平人，山东科技大学副教授、硕士生导师，美国匹兹堡大学访问学者，山东省作家协会会员。2018 年开始写诗，诗文见诸报端。用旅行、阅读、电影、写作来对抗生命的虚妄。

邮箱：towanghua@163.com

献给我的姥姥，夏庆芳女士

Dedicated to my grandma, Mrs. Xia Qingfang

献给爱我和我爱的人

To those who love me and to whom I love

序　言

　　读罢王华诗集《海未央》，首先想到的是诗集名字起得挺好，显然受《诗经》的影响，"夜如何其？夜未央，庭燎之光。"（《诗经·小雅》）然后想到的是《给青年诗人的十封信》中的里尔克和青年诗人。里尔克在给这位青年诗人的第一封信中指出："你的诗没有自己的特点，虽然暗中也静静地潜伏着向着个性发展的趋势。"里尔克还让他回答一个重要问题："在夜深最寂静的时刻问问自己：我必须写吗？你要在自身内挖掘一个深的答复。"王华与这位青年诗人在某些方面有相似之处，同样她也需要回答"我必须写吗？"这个问题。我知道王华一定会毫不犹豫地说："是的，我必须写。"因为她有一种对诗歌"清教徒"式的虔诚，一种对诗歌一往情深的不懈追求，一种没有诗歌的陪伴，生活就寡淡无味，生命就失去色彩的执念。

　　是的，我对王华的印象就是如此。她对文学的热爱超乎寻常，颇似 20 世纪 80 年代的文学青年，相形于当下青年与文学的疏离，反差感强烈。我常在塔楼 1901 良友书坊的作家新书分享活动上见到她，她总是凝神倾听作家发言，而且她从西海岸驾车穿越海底隧道到良友书坊，单程需要一个小时。每每如此，不免令人感动于心。在我们举办的"首届青岛诗歌节暨国际海洋文学周"活动中，她和小西陪同著名诗人胡弦游览崂山。胡弦在写青岛的一首诗《秋日下午，崂山行》中写道："回城的路上，王华一直在问我：哪些人的诗写得好？我胡乱地说着一些名字。其实，我在看海，和悬崖上不断闪退的树。"王华为她的名字进入胡弦的诗而开心和感恩，由此看出她对诗歌的热爱到了无以复加的程度。

王华在山东科技大学工作。我三年前受邀为山东科技大学校庆作品集写序时，曾读过她的两篇颇具学者风格的散文，印象深刻。其中一篇《"邂逅"三位美国"总统"》，是写她 2016 年在美国访学时于匹兹堡大学演讲厅看到拜登、在匹兹堡大学老兵纪念馆遇见特朗普、在卡内基·梅隆大学遥看希拉里演讲的感受。文章透露出她广博的见识和学问。另一篇《书香是永恒的守护》则写她阅读大量经典作品，从米沃什、帕斯和荷尔德林专业性极强的诗歌佳作，到极难懂的哲学著作，诸多感悟随想，可谓思想深刻、眼界辽阔。

诗集《海未央》呈现出王华诗歌创作的新面貌，可将其概括为三个主要特征。

一、双语是诗的密钥

《海未央》是一本汉英双语诗集。王华似乎意识到自己精通英语的优势，用汉语和英语同时创作一首诗。这一优势，不容小觑。一个在母语之外掌握一门外语的人，在语言的大厦里站得更高，看得更远。诗歌是极致的语言艺术，如此可以领会不同语言之间、词语与词语组合的不同效果和微妙差异所带来的意外之意。这是在母语的封闭系统中如何"念咒"也难以实现和体味的。我甚至认为双语有时是诗的密钥，她能引领我们抵达母语的边界，触摸和打开语言神秘的界门，跨越难以逾越的界线。从王华的双语诗中我们能约略看出这种端倪，比如第3首诗："我的蓝色恋人 / 我们之间不写信件 / 也不需要电联 / 你的眼眸，有我想要的所有深情。"最后一句用英语表达是"Your eyes give all the affection I want"，显然这句诗的英语版比汉语版更有诗意。"eyes give all the affection"采用拟人修辞的英语表述，与汉语版的微妙差异强化了它的诗意。再如第6首："任何心境我都想凝望大海 / 一个私密的对话框 / 倒空自己，而后满载而归。"其中"倒空自己，而后满载而归"的英文是"Empty myself, then come back fully loaded"。虽然都是Paradox（悖论）的表达手段，但是可以看出汉语"满载而归"远不及英语"come back fully loaded"的诗意效果。

反之亦然，英语诗句不如汉语的表达更有诗意也是相同的逻辑。比如第13首："试着抛出旧伤和新疼／看它们淹没在下一次波涛里／潮涨潮落如同刮骨疗伤／我像鱼一样沉潜／一次次在潮汐里修行。"其中"潮涨潮落如同刮骨疗伤"的英文是"Ebb and flow is like shaving the bone for healing"，相比较当然还是汉语的诗意更高级。再如较为典型的第59首"我在四月幻想一场热恋／潮水一点点退回安全地带／对于陆地总是浅尝辄止／听说那儿过于危险"。其中"对于陆地总是浅尝辄止"的英语"Always cursory to the land"远不如汉语有诗意。《海未央》中类似这种汉英语言对照形成的诗意反差俯拾皆是，很好诠释了掌握一门外语的重要性。

二、以海为母体的新态势

住在海边的诗人心中总有个大海，激越与平静、潮起与潮落、切近与辽远，他们举手投足之间透着海的颜色、气息和辽阔。王华每天都在大海的视野中徜徉，西海岸的海平静时宛若处子，疯狂时如脱缰野马，诗人的激情总会被它点燃，迸发出具有海洋性格、海洋气息的诗句。诗集《海未央》就是一本自然之海与内心之海相互叠加的大海之诗，也可视其为一首以海洋为母体的长诗。

海，辽阔无垠，看上去空无一物。岛屿也孤独，轮船也寂寞。面对难以言说的虚无，如何创造言之有物的诗歌，这是诗人们尝试开垦的蓝色土地。王华以其特有的视角"任何心境我都想凝望大海"，与大海这个"私密的对话框"对话，思考爱情的真谛、人性的隐秘、社会的难题、历史的真伪。然后以格言警句风格的诗歌呈现瞬间和永恒的诗意盛开。如第5首就是以爱情、人性和社会关联为主题的一首诗。"千万人口的都市／没有人爱他／他时常驻足于海边／仿佛因此可以融入鱼群。"在人口如此稠密的城市却得不到哪怕一个人的爱，这样的人在海边显得多么孤单，以致他想离开人群，融入另一个种群——鱼群。如此决绝的选择，如此凄冷的孤独，让人感同身受。第17首则是以爱情为主题的诗。"那个失恋的男子／把匕首插入大海／试图刺穿它的骨头。"男子，失恋的男子，把匕首刺入大海，刺穿大海的骨头，而不是他物。作为爱情诗，王华能写出如此有力量的诗句，可以说颇有创造力。第25首是写人性的一首诗。"他一个人看海／阳光将影子拉长／一只鸟在弹性的枝条上颤动／似乎有着抖不落的悲哀。"一位男子在海边的孤独，比孤独还孤独；一只鸟在他的孤独上跳来跳去，树枝颤动了他深入骨髓的孤独。采用一人一鸟的互文性写作，来表现人类孤独的诗也颇具独特性。第 62 首则是一首以死亡为主题的沉重的诗。"漏风的房子搭在黄土一样的洞里萨湖 / 夜推开沉重的门 / 一堆枯叶落到纸上 / 死亡都没有一丝声音。"推开沉重的死亡之门，失去生命的枯叶落在空白或白纸黑字的纸上，轻轻地，没有声音。人的消失，万物的消亡不皆如此吗？同时，这首诗也体现了诗人对弱势群体、对世间生灵的悲悯之心。

三、以表达自然、人生哲理见长

作为给大学生讲授西方文学的学者，一些常见的写作手法，王华也一定了然于心。她的诗展开推进大多是通过象征、暗喻、夸张、互文、对比等手法实现的，而这些手法、技巧和诗歌意象又都围绕着她所思考的人生哲理。比如第 18 首："在青岛，时常看不到海 / 雾气浓厚绵长 / 像一些人的面具 / 摘不下来。"这里的"面具"暗喻浮躁时代的人与人之间的复杂关系，让人看不清海也看不清人，更看不清世界。第 21 首诗则写围海造田，既有主体对科技、环保的反思，又有客体被伤害、反噬主体的危机意识："人们把海水切割成湾畔 / 被围困的野兽 / 体内有再多的怒火 / 也无法形成滔天巨浪。"第 61 首揭示了自然、人和社会作为一个"矛盾体"中的不可避免的疑惑、猜忌与冲突的人类困囿："海上的风从未停歇／阳光笑里藏刀／白天和黑夜的边界模糊／开灯时间越来越长"。阳光的光芒刺眼如刀，白天和黑夜的边界模糊，其象征性不言而喻。

可以说诗集《海未央》是王华诗歌攀升的一个新高度，标志着她的诗歌正走向成熟的"麦地"，走向辽阔的"大海"。而她左手汉语，右手英语，能够随心所欲切换、自由自在行走，这又为她的诗歌插上"鹰"的翅膀。我们期待这只"鹰"越飞越高，越过草原、河流、高山和大海，成为天之骄子。让我们拭目以待。

高建刚

2024.12.18

Listening to the sound of the sea

The journey of modern Chinese poetry began in the early 20th century, influenced by the May Fourth Movement and Western literary trends. Poets such as Hu Shi, Xu Zhimo and Ai Qing, began to break away from classical forms, embracing free verse and vernacular language to express personal emotions and social commentary. This shift allowed for greater accessibility and relevance to the general public, making poetry a powerful medium for reflection and change. Wang Hua's poetry is a point of contemporary Chinese poetry and contains a wealth of information about this development and change.

Born, raised and worked by the sea, Wang Hua's *The Boundless Sea* has an overall image of the sea, and when she wants to express herself through poetry as a literary style, the image of the sea becomes the most appropriate carrier, just like Tao Yuanming's *Peach Blossom Garden* and Henry David Thoreau's *Walden*. Sea and waves are among the most important and frequent keywords of *The Boundless Sea*, and they are powerful and evocative symbols, often representing vastness, mystery, and the depth of human emotions. This reminds me of Persian poetry, for example, poets like Rumi (as my favorite poet) and Hafez often draw on the sea's vastness to express the boundless nature of remarkable love and spiritual quests. Rumi: "The sea is a drop in the divine ocean, and the ocean is a drop in the sea." This line illustrates the interconnection of the divine and the universe, emphasizing the infinite nature of both.

Also in Chinese poetry, the sea often symbolizes the boundaries of the known world and the spirit of exploration. It is also a source of inspiration and reflection, as seen in the works of poets like Li Bai and Cao Cao. "Tides of the spring river wash into the leveled ocean, and with the tide, a luminous moon is born above the sea surface." This imagery from Zhang Ruoxu's poem highlights the sea's connection to the natural world and its role in the cycle of life.

As is clear, both Persian and Chinese poets use the

sea to explore themes of infinity, mystery, and the human condition. The sea's ever-changing nature serves as a powerful metaphor for life's journey, filled with challenges and transformations. These shared themes highlight the universal appeal of the sea as a literary symbol, transcending cultural boundaries and resonating deeply with readers across different traditions.

I met Wang Hua, a young Chinese Associate Professor, in the fall of 2023 in the beautiful city of Qingdao at the World Sinology Center. At that time, I had traveled to China on behalf of my country Iran and the University of Tehran as a member of the board of trustees of this center, and I was excited about the wide capacities of comparative studies between Persian and Chinese civilizations.

Nobel Prize-winning Chilean poet Neruda said, "There are only two things that are indispensable in life: poetry and love." In *The Boundless Sea*, Wang Hua uses a unique female perspective to focus on nature, love, loneliness, birds, waves, rocks, and the underprivileged. All the philosophical imagery about the sea fits the experience and literacy of a scholar. Yes, a poet must be sensitive, and be a worshipper of nature. In almost every poem, Wang

Hua employs such rhetorical devices as metaphor, symbolism, hyperbole, personification, paradox, to express a genuine experience of existence and compassion.

The fact that *The Boundless Sea* is presented in both Chinese and English is a significant capacity for better understanding of the concepts and of course the comparative study of translation between two languages and two cultures. It can also be used as a learning example of Chinese poetry going overseas. I believe it is seldomly to see Chinese poets who can write and translate in both Chinese and English.

The Boundless Sea is both a code for individual lives and, in some cases, a response to the reality of Chinese society. It offers insights into Chinese culture, history and social values. It contributes to both Chinese and global literary traditions. I think Wang Hua's *The Boundless Sea* will be considered one of the contemporary works of China in this field. I hope you enjoy reading this book as much as I do.

Hamed Vafaei

2024.12.8

海未央

×

The Boundless Sea

No. 1.

Lakes and rivers, these scattered children

Some are active, some quiet

Both inherited the dark blue pupils of their father

湖泊和河流这些散落四处的孩子
有的好动，有的文静
都继承了父亲深蓝色的眼眸

No 2.

I always accompany the choppy sea

The world is tough, and the sea never freezes

That is why my heart has no scars

我常常陪着大海波涛汹涌
世事艰难，它从不结冰
我的心因此也没有伤痕

No 3.

My beloved blue sea

There is no correspondence between us

And no phone calls

Your eyes give all the affection I want

我的蓝色恋人

我们之间不写信件

也不需要电联

你的眼眸，有我想要的所有深情

The cross-sea Metro Line 1

Through the heart of Jiaozhou Bay

Faster than our life and love

Getting off any time in case of a wrong direction

跨海地铁 1 号线
在胶州湾的心脏穿行
比我们的生活和爱情还快
方向错误，也可以随时下车

N°. 5.

Nobody loves him

In a city of ten million people

He always stands by the sea

As if he would lose himself in the school of fish

千万人口的都市
没有人爱他
他时常驻足于海边
仿佛因此可以融入鱼群

I gaze at the sea in any state of mind

A private dialog box

Empty myself, then come back fully loaded

任何心境我都想凝望大海

一个私密的对话框

倒空自己，而后满载而归

Tangdao Bay is heavily foggy

The sea hangs upside down in the sky

Like love which makes one dizzy

唐岛湾大雾磅礴

海倒挂在天空

和让人眩晕的爱情一模一样

There are no problems that the sea may not solve

Once diluted

Anything will fade

没有什么问题是大海解决不了的
一稀释
都会变淡

N°.9.

I watch the sea as much as I give lectures
During the lectures, I am always talking
While with the sea, I am listening

我看海的时间和讲课一样多
课堂上，我在说话
看海时，我在聆听

The sea is not always clear

Sometimes like cataracts of the elderly

With a kind of unclean cloudiness

海并不总是清澈

有时像得了白内障

带着一种擦不干净的浑浊

Meeting you is like a smog

A small boat is to hit the rock

Corrected by the storm in time

遇见你是一场烟雾
一艘即将触礁的小船
被风暴及时纠正了航向

The wind loosens its grip

So the wrinkles of the sea disappear

He hides himself in the depths of the season

And the mornings never come again afterwards

风松开手

海的皱纹就消失了

他躲在季节深处

从此，早晨也不再来

Tentatively throw out the old wounds and new pains
Watch them being drowned in the next wave
Ebb and flow is like shaving the bone for healing
I dive like a fish
Cultivating myself with tides over and over again

试着抛出旧伤和新疼

看它们淹没在下一次波涛里

潮涨潮落如同刮骨疗伤

我像鱼一样沉潜

一次次在潮汐里修行

The old man always basks himself in the corner

Time is stiff

Only the waves are passing by in front of his eyes

老人总是躲在角落晒太阳

时光僵硬

只有一波波的浪花从眼前流过

Like a splash of red wine

The sunset over the sea is magnificent

A wild horse does not know the way home

I retreat to my own shore quietly

如同泼洒了一杯红酒
海上落日壮阔
一匹野马不知道回家的路
我默然退回自己的岸边

The promise of the wind is always flighty

And the sea stays steady as a rock

It is never swayed by sweet words

Though its skin is cut crisscross

风的承诺，总是轻飘飘的
大海稳若磐石
从来不被甜言蜜语灌得东倒西歪
即使肌肤被划成阡陌纵横的路

The lovelorn man

Thrusts his dagger into the sea

Trying to pierce its bones

那个失恋的男子
把匕首插入大海
试图刺穿它的骨头

The sea is always unseeable in Qingdao

Owing to the heavy fog

Like the mask worn by people

Hard to take it off

在青岛，时常看不到海
雾气浓厚绵长
像一些人的面具
摘不下来

The summer sea is extremely humid

Making a city blossom with the rain

As if disappointed in a romance

夏天的海，无比潮湿氤氲
让一座城市梨花带雨
像是制造一场失恋

In the hard times

I carry the sea forward

The blue keeps following

Like a gentleman of noble blood

艰难的岁月里

我背着海走

蓝色一直跟随

如同一位血统高贵的绅士

People cut the seawater into bays

The besieged beasts

In spite of the burning anger inside

Could not make monstrous waves anymore

人们把海水切割成湾畔
被围困的野兽
体内有再多的怒火
也无法形成滔天巨浪

No 22.

My love seems to have slept for thousands of years

Its ethereal form

At the bottom of the deep ocean

Still radiating a strong light tenaciously

我的爱好像沉睡了上千年
它气若游丝的魅影
在幽深的海底
依然顽强地放射光芒

Walking from flowering to petals falling

Spring is missed, and autumn is to be missed too

If the sea is filled with fog

How do I recognize his traces

从花开走到花落

错过了春天，也即将错过秋天

如果海上浓雾四起

我该如何辨认他的足迹

If you come back from afar

The day we meet

The wind is blowing the petals

A fragrant pathway is paved on the sea

你如果从远方归来

相聚的那天

风鼓着花瓣

在海上铺成一条芳香的甬道

No. 25.

He watches the sea alone

The sun lengthens the shadow

A bird quivers on an elastic branch

A kind of sadness seems hard to shed off

他一个人看海

阳光将影子拉长

一只鸟在弹性的枝条上颤动

似乎有着抖不落的悲哀

She is always heading for the blue when painful

The limitless expanse

So similar to countless lives without an exit

她总是在疼痛的时候走向一片蓝
那找不到边际的辽阔
和无数个没有出口的人生那么相似

The setting sun sinks into the depths of the ocean

Like a girl infatuated with love

Renewed only after the baptism of the night

落日在海洋深处沉沦

如同被爱情冲昏头脑的女子

经过黑夜的洗礼，才能焕发新生

The wind always tries to break the calm

To sprinkle a little emotion into the air

Under repeated pestering

No wave will seal the heart of love

风总是试图打破平静

将一些小小的情绪推波助澜

反复纠缠之下

没有一朵浪花能够封心锁爱

The waves hit the rock again and again

Like the temptation of love

Splattering all over her without any response

海浪一次次叩打岩石

像是爱情的试探

得不到回应

就溅湿她一身

Typhoons occasionally pass through Qingdao
Laoshan Mountain is a magic cudgel
With the will of Odysseus
To resist the temptation of Siren's song

台风偶尔途经青岛
崂山是一枚定海神针
用奥德修斯的意志
抵抗塞壬①歌声的诱惑

---

①塞壬，希腊神话中人身鸟足的海妖，她常以天籁般的歌声诱惑过路的航海者，使航船触礁沉没。奥德修斯用蜡封住同伴们的耳朵，又让同伴们用绳索将自己绑在船桅上，方才安然渡过。

Without rippling secrets

The sky is an ocean of tranquility

Far from the earth

And away from all the rights and wrongs

没有跌宕起伏的秘密

天空是一片宁静的海

远离大地

也就远离了一切是非恩怨

Lovesickness opens up in every morning

Not only to think of you in dreams

My verses are overgrown with nameless grasses

Silent as the rising sea

思念开放在每一个清晨
想你不仅仅是在梦中
我的诗句种满无名的草
沉默着如同涨潮的海

Fishes play among the lotus leaves

Coveting those enchanting water plants

The lake is unusually calm

Ancient ripples have been smoothed by the years

鱼儿在荷叶间嬉戏

觊觎那些妖娆的水草

湖面异常平静

古老的波澜早已被岁月安抚如新

The muddy Yellow River meanders along

Through the better part of China

Grown up, I come to know

It is the color of suffering in the blood

泥土般的黄河蜿蜒而下
途经大半个中国
长大后才明白
那是血液里苦难的颜色

It seems I watched a movie with the air

My heart is barren

Looking for love in an age of restlessness

Like waiting for a flower to bloom at the sea

我好像是和空气看完一场电影
内心一片荒芜
在浮躁的时代寻找爱情
如同在海上期待一朵花开

Never floated on Wind-fire Rings when I was young

Always known the difficulties of rooted in the earth

The candies received were so colorful and varied

Still knowing the one wrapped in sweet bitterness

年少时未曾踩着风火轮在云端漂浮

一直深知这扎根大地的困厄

收到的糖果缤纷冗杂

依然可以分辨哪颗包裹着甜的苦涩

White cats are soft as if they had no bones

Like water to cope with the hard world

I walk from north to south

A straightforward person, writing abstract poetry

白猫柔软到好像没有骨骼

水一般应对坚硬的世界

我从北走到南

一个直率的人，写留白的诗

No 38.

Mom always tattooed her scars with flowers

The sun has cleared up a bit

While she is getting smaller

A narrowing and thinning stream

Could not hold the ups and downs of her destiny

妈妈总是把伤疤刻上花朵

太阳晴朗了一些

她越来越小

一条变窄变瘦的溪流

装不下她命运的起伏

She is as humble as water

Looking after a corner of the earth for a lifetime

The light in the eyes of her children

To soothe the pains in her

她如水一样谦卑
一生照看土地一隅
孩子眼里的光
减轻身体里的疼

A rope is like the iron tongs of life

Firmly tethering the drifting wooden boat

Faced with the tough waves

Without weightlessness and sinking

一条绳索如同生活的铁钳
牢牢拴住飘摇的木船
让它在惊涛骇浪面前
不至于失重和沉沦

The Mid-Autumn moon is pouring over the sea

To sprinkle fairly on everyone

Her sorrow is suddenly relieved

As if she has been comforted by love

中秋的月光倾泻海面

公平地洒到每个人身上

她突然没有那么悲伤

像是刚刚被爱情抚慰了一番

As I gaze upon you

Stars spread over the sea

The speedboat draws a rainbow

Thousands of seagulls are whispering

Building a white bridge

我望着你

星星洒满海面

快艇画出一条彩虹

千万只海鸥窃窃私语

搭起一座白色的桥

N⁰ 43.

The waves are trapped by rocks sometimes
After struggling
They disappear into the sea

海浪有时会被岩石锁住咽喉

挣扎过后

只能销声匿迹

The sea is a mirror

The undulating love story with the sun

Like the process of conceiving a poem

大海是一面镜子
和太阳起起落落的爱情故事
犹如构思一首诗的过程

The curtain of the night, still and quiet

The sea is silent at last

Like a tired child

The inner noise is temporarily covered by the night

夜幕阒寂无声

海终于沉寂下来

像一个玩累的孩童

内心的喧嚣，暂时被黑夜覆盖

It is not always the daytime tea keeping me awake
It could be the birds fluttering their wings at sea
I always feel they have some truth to tell

有时候让我无法入睡的
不一定是白天的茶
也可能是海上不停扇动翅膀的鸟儿
总觉得它们有些真相要诉说

The vastness and depths of the sea floor

No longer shake direction of a breath of the wind

I finally learnt to be silent

Not remembering your name anymore

海底的苍茫与幽深
再也撼动不了一丝风的走向
我终于学会了沉默
已记不起你的名字

Birds who do not associate with humans

Still chirping among the bare branches

Like a candle in the sea

Which breaks the long silence

不与人类亲近的鸟儿
还在光秃的枝丫间啁啾
像是大海里的烛火
打碎长久的沉默

I pack the mountains and rivers into my bag

When I am sad

I hide myself in my cave

Cutting off a small corner

To taste

我把山水打包到行囊

忧伤的时候

躲进自己的洞穴

切出一个小角

品尝

No. 50.

Love that decays quickly is like foam on the beach
Qarhan Salt Lake
Before love gets old
Seals it in transparent amber

速朽的爱，像沙滩留下的浮沫

察尔汗盐湖

在爱情还没有变老之前

把它封存成通透的琥珀

Ocean mends its wound only during fishing moratorium

When it was about to heal, it was torn apart

Some people are forever demanding and requiring

To harvest gifts of all sorts

Before it is empty

海洋只能在休渔期缝补伤口
快要愈合时又被伤到体无完肤
有人永远在索取
收获形形色色的礼物
在它还没有被掏空的时候

N<u>o</u> 52.

The sea stands mute under the cover of night
I still dare not do anything evil
When the sun is rising
I do not feel guilty

夜幕下的海，万马齐喑
我仍然不敢胡作非为
等日出的时候
才不会感到愧疚

Waking up in the morning

I do not know where to place my heart

The empty wind and I keep our respective thoughts

Are still waiting

早晨醒来

心不知道放在哪里

空荡荡的风和我各怀心事

还在等待

When you are drowning

I fish you out

Your breath soaks the words

It makes my book a little bit heavier

溺水时
我把你打捞上来
你的呼吸浸湿一个个文字
我的书因此厚重了一些

Time holds a torch

To illuminate some

To leave some out

No strength to throw myself out like a fishing rod

时光举着火把

照亮一些

也遗漏一些

已经没有力气像鱼竿一样甩出自己

Lovesickness is like the sea

His hieroglyphs have since become a pile of paper

Scattered in the jungle where no one else can reach

The sunlight wanders lonely

The shadow of the trees is imagining a person

相思如海

他的象形文字从此成为一堆纸

散落在别人到不了的丛林

阳光寂寞流浪

树影在想象一个人的模样

N<u>o</u> 57.

You say the weather is hot and cold

As changeable as the times now

After the wind blows

It hurts anywhere

你说天气忽冷忽热
像当下的时代一样多变
风吹过后
哪里都痛

The clouds are getting thicker and deeper

To cover all sides like a hat

A stranded fish is never able to return to its harbor

云层越来越厚重低沉
帽子一样覆盖四周
一条搁浅的鱼
再也回不到最初的港湾

I fantasize about a passionate love in April
The tide gradually recedes to safety of the sea
Always cursory to the land
It is said to be too dangerous

我在四月幻想一场热恋
潮水一点点退回安全地带
对于陆地总是浅尝辄止
听说那儿过于危险

The sunshine can not dry up

the dampness and darkness inside you

When will you look no higher than your head

Start to care about the land and the food

To feel the sadness of a fish

阳光晒不干你体内的潮湿和阴暗
什么时候你的目光才不会高于头顶
开始关心土地和粮食
感知一条鱼的悲伤

No. 61.

The wind never stops at the sea
Sunshine hides a knife in its smile
The boundary between day and night is blurred
Lights are turned on longer and longer

海上的风从未停歇
阳光笑里藏刀
白天和黑夜的边界模糊
开灯时间越来越长

N⁰ 62.

Leaky houses are built over yellow Tonle Sap Lake
Night pushes the heavy door open
A pile of dead leaves fall onto the paper
Death does not even make a sound

漏风的房子搭在黄土一样的洞里萨湖①

夜推开沉重的门

一堆枯叶落到纸上

死亡都没有一丝声音

---

①洞里萨湖，被称为"柬埔寨的心脏"，是东南亚最大的淡水湖。据说一些越南难民的后裔，为躲避战争，逃难到此。后来越南视他们为叛国者，柬埔寨也不接纳他们，所以他们只能住在湖上。他们世世代代没有国籍，房屋漂浮在湖中，形成万人左右的"水上村寨"。

No. 63.

Fireworks explode in the night sky over Pittsbrugh
A baby like an angel from Syria smiles at me
The moment she was born into the world
She saw the fireworks like gunfire

烟花在匹兹堡夜空华丽绽放
来自叙利亚的婴儿朝我微笑，美若天使
她刚降临人间
就看到炮火一样的烟花

The Gulf of Mexico on the left
The Atlantic Ocean on the right
Under Miami Route One
Embrace each other as if nobody is watching

左边墨西哥湾

右边大西洋

在迈阿密一号公路之下

旁若无人般深情相拥

后记

　　诗集付梓之际，好像是把最心爱的礼物交付出去，等待它与世界见面，内心平静又欢欣。

　　至今还记得那个美妙的日子。我偶然看到2018年青岛元宵诗会征稿，随手写了首诗，通过邮箱发过去。第二天一早就收到邀约。一周之后，32位获奖的老中青诗人相聚在良友书坊。诗会上，主持人邵竹君玉树临风，诗情澎湃。大家上台朗读自己的诗作，或低吟，或激扬，深情又投入，诗意翩飞。那一天，我深深感受到新诗的魅力，当晚在朋友圈发文："我懵懂地闯进一场华丽诗会。给我一个十年，以梦为马，与诗共年华。"写诗的种子，自此萌芽。从那之后，我又陆续参加了樱花诗会和中秋诗会等。

　　工作需要，有时候我也给大学生讲解《英美文学》，其中的诗歌部分，当然也令人着迷。英国的莎士比亚、邓恩、华兹华斯、拜伦、雪莱、济慈、托马斯、勃朗宁夫妇、哈代、叶芝、艾略特、休斯等，美国的惠特曼、狄金森、弗罗斯特、史蒂文斯、庞德、卡明斯、普拉斯等都是课堂的常客。如果文学素养深厚，万物皆可入诗。比如莎士比亚的第18首十四行诗。英伦夏季的天气最舒适，因此有"June Bride"（六月新娘）一说。诗人将心爱之人比作美妙夏日，随后回答：尽管你比夏日更温婉更可爱。一问一答，就有道不完的美好情愫，也和苏轼的"欲把西湖比西子，浓妆淡抹总相宜"有着异曲同工之妙。讲着讲着，我时常会听见内心愈发强烈的声音：为什么不自己写诗呢？

然而，读诗、讲诗与写诗隔着千山万水的距离。写诗的道路并不顺畅，要写出一首好诗更是艰难，相信严肃的诗人都感同身受。于是我买来大量国外优秀诗人的作品，认真研读。阿多尼斯、里尔克、米沃什、帕斯、荷尔德林、塞弗尔特、佩索阿、洛尔迦、达菲、布罗茨基、特朗斯特罗姆、曼德尔施塔姆、扎加耶夫斯基、帕斯捷尔纳克、阿赫马托娃等诗人的佳作一度占据着我书架上最显眼的位置……虽然阿多尼斯认为其最重要的作品是长诗，但其短诗也依然出色。

《你的眼睛和我之间》

当我把眼睛沉入你的眼睛
我瞥见幽深的黎明

我看到古老的昨天

看到我不能领悟的一切

我感到宇宙正在流动

在你的眼睛和我之间

第一次读到这首诗时，我就深受震撼。彼此凝视的瞬间，一个光彩绚烂的星空，一片深沉无边的海洋，所有的一切，神秘的和浪漫的，都正在发生。好诗的魅力无以言表，一语千金，意蕴深长。这些一流的优秀诗作可以帮助新手从最初就避开一些浅漏的陷阱，从而保持高标准、高姿态的自我要求。所谓"取乎其上，得乎其中；取乎其中，得乎其下；取乎其下，则无所得矣"，正如此。有一段时间，我也在想，如果20世纪80年代的人在青少年时代就有机会习读世界一流诗人的佳作，或许人生会多一些选择。

当然，我也读国内诗人的佳作，从北岛、顾城、海子、舒婷、昌耀、张枣，到西川、欧阳江河、翟永明、胡弦、大解、李元胜等。我还有缘得以与其中一些人在青岛相见，聆听他们的讲座，那真是一段无比欢快惬意的时光。

有了情绪，就会写诗。一路走来，收获了很多善意的鼓励和肯定。青岛美丽绵长的黄金海岸线也给予我写诗的灵感和生活的哲思。感谢高伟、周蓬桦和刘涛的推荐语。非常感谢南开大学教授、翻译家张智中和美国麻省理工学院教授、汉学家张仲思（Tristan Brown）对英译部分的认真审校。郑重感谢伊朗德黑兰大学教授、汉学家好麦特（Hamed Vafaei）的英文序言，从他优美的语言中，我收获了很多。特别感谢原青岛市作协主席高建刚，他牵线承办高品位的诗歌节，邀请重量级的诗人来青岛交流；感恩他真诚且有见地的序言。感谢诗人、小说家、画家张毅，慷慨奉献精美画作。感谢我的姥姥夏庆芳女士，她虽逝去多年，但从未真正离开。这位美丽了一生、优雅了一生的女子，是我生命中永恒的精神坐标。感谢我的血亲，他们深沉厚重的爱让我有力量面对世间所有的风雨与磨砺。

诺贝尔文学奖得主、墨西哥诗人帕斯在诺贝尔颁奖仪式上说："诗歌特别钟爱瞬间，并愿意在一首诗中重温那个时刻，将它从延续中分离出来，并将它变成固定的现时。"所以，如果有缘，希望你也能在某个瞬间，把眼睛沉入我的诗行。

幸好，这世界还有诗歌。有你，有我。

王 华

2024 年 10 月 25 日写于青岛